MANCHESTER ARMS

RICK EDELSTEIN

ISBN: 978-1-988827-50-6

Scarlet Leaf Publishing House
2016

Manchester Arms

Scarlet Leaf Publishing House has allowed this work to remain exactly as the author intended.

Rick Edelstein

DEDICATION

To Rumi who does open heart surgery on this
positive nihilist.

Manchester Arms

I knew it would be a problem for them. My Mother made no effort to hide her indignant vexed self-glancing at me discursively and blowing on her tea. (Conundrum: We blow on hot tea to cool and cold hands to warm.) She sipped, nodded approbation, put the cup down, folded her arms over maternal breasts (of course a mother's breasts are maternal) as she proactively stared me down in a demanding almost-silence. Almost, as incoherent sounds emanated beyond vocabulary. It was a familiar pose intended to intimidate which worked when I was younger but now, well, her accusatory silence had little effect as I have developed a selective sense of hearing even to her assertive judgmental tsk tsking.

Imposing or perhaps commenting on

Mother's censorious silence was the tick-tock (there really is a tock) of the kitchen clock (rhyme not intended.) Looking at the clock with its porcelain ballet dancers moving in an unending circle reminded me of a pun I made calling it a kitsch-en clock but no one got it, particularly Father who gifted this clock to my Mother as an anniversary present. Although I wonder if that unending circular move, like the Buddhist wheel which has no beginning or end, I wonder if those dancing figurines might be revered by some yet-to-be-discovered culture of ancient Albinos whose tribe was interred during the preferred plagues in Southern France [I am not a fan of the French who philosophize and hide in a closet while others do the fighting.]

I was grounded out of my dystopian fantasy by Father who was noisily moving objects on the red and white checkerboard patterned tablecloth as if playing chess but I knew, as did he and my Mother, that he was waiting for his wife, the Mother of his son, to take the lead. And as big Will said, "The world is a stage and we are but the players in it," Mom took the cue, adjusted a strand of her graying hair which was not out of place, chewed a moment on her lower lip which was—if you were a professional poker player—a clear 'tell' indicating a substantial hand was about to be played.

"I can't believe it. Four years of college,"

My Father triumphantly pushed the saltshaker onto a red square, looked up at me as if he had my king pinned, "For which I paid..."

Mom perfectly harmonizing their practiced 34-year duet, "We paid most definitely, we did, indeed!"

And Dad did his redundant eighth notes pizzicato, "Full tuition, no student loan mind you, no scholarship for Mason William Harrison's son. No sir. We pay for what we choose and demand suitable return on our investment. Yes sir."

I transformed us into the ideally prepared trio playing my part as I mellifluously glissando'd,

"I was offered a scholarship based on my…"

Father slammed the pepper mill down on a white square, accenting the move with a no-doubt-about-it severe tonal force-field detonation, "This family does not take handouts!" (And he did end with an exclamation point.)

He turned to my Mother as if awaiting affirmation, which she yielded with a vigorous nod of the head, her glasses slightly slipping down the bridge of her substantial nose, "Thank you. And for what? My son a college graduate…" She leaned her head toward Dad as if she was Beyoncé about to bust a move or rather her generation would be closer to Sarah Vaughan ending her plaintive chorus leaving space for him to play a few chords, which of course he recognized and accepted con brio.

"Honors graduate!" Playing a blues bass line, Dad folded and refolded the matching red and white cloth napkin until it was perfectly aligned to his satisfaction, leaned back with a tilt toward his wife, who picked up the chord progression.

Nodding in almost two-four time, Mom hit the high hat, "…is going to be a bell-boy."

The tune ended with no resolution. I was ready, willing and eager to egress up up and away but I knew they were exchanging their metaphorical instruments for something that might transmogrify into an aggressive duet bludgeoning me more severely. There was no defense in an arena not of my choosing. I remained stridently silent which was not to my Father's liking. He was armed, ready for battle but could not retaliate if the enemy was on hiatus. Nevertheless he threw out the tempting salvo, "Boy, hmmph. You're what, twenty-one, legal, qualified for everything including choices. Choices young man, at twenty one you have…"

He knows my age and my mumbled response was a feint indicating that I made the choice not to engage, "Two months shy of twenty-two."

Mother osmosed into the rhythm of the

attack prodding me toward the playing field as only a Mother can, "Just hear out your Father, Sonny."

And Father picked up his cue, "I taught you and lest you forget, Lawrence Dunbar Harrison, we do not make an effort to fit in, we stand out, and proudly, I taught you that we do not, I repeat, not change our behavior or adjust our countenance to make other people comfortable regardless of their race, gender or position. I taught you better than to allow anyone to call you boy!" Daddy trumped swiftly.

No longer quietly offering information but now biting the hook of the cliché generation busting a cap in the gap, "I am not a bell boy. I am a Courtesy Assistant, why do you keep insisting that I am…"

Mom gave me no room to breathe, "Semantics. My son choosing to work as a bell…"

I was not accommodating, "Courtesy Assistant, not bell boy, but a man, a Courtesy

Assistant which will appear on my paycheck, Lawrence Dunbar Harrison, Courtesy Assistant, period."

And of course Dad pulled rank with a vocal body slam that promised superior bravado if unheeded, "Change your tone when talking to your mother!"

Mother - securely defended by her West Indian man-warrior - in a softened pitch to her first-born, adjusted her glasses, looked at me with the polarity of love and disapproval, "Why, Sonny, just tell me why, give me one good reason why you actually choose to work at some tawdry hotel in a position for which you are eminently over-qualified?"

"To say the least," Father clichéd.

I, too, softened, in a voice soliciting reason, appreciation and support, "As a matter of fact, Mom, The Manchester Arms is a very expensive, exclusive, residential hotel with residents, well some of whom have been and are very active in the media, politics and others who are related to substantial well-connected people in the corporate and entertainment fields. There isn't even a name on the outside and yet there is a waiting list for reserve suites and…"

Father did not like the direction the game was going and tried to redraw the familiar line in the sand, "You're not answering your Mother's question, Lawrence. Why, I repeat, why should you, a college graduate who purportedly has or had aspirations to be a writer although you showed a proclivity on the piano and your Mother a fine pianist in her own right and I'm not too shabby on reeds…"

Mother assuaged, "Your sound is a combination of Stan Getz and Lester Young."

Father played the shy act not very well, "From your mouth to God's ear…and you Son, we thought you might become a composer, for God's sakes you..."

"Don't blaspheme, Mason."

"Well he did make the honor roll in high school leading the school band in jazz classics not just the standards."

"You're right there, Mason," Mom intoned making peace with the man she just criticized which he received with an appreciative humph. "Your father's observations demand attention, Lawrence. For heaven's sakes in contrast to most boys of your generation you actually loved Mozart, Bach..."

Dad jumped in with proud enthusiasm, "And Miles, all the kids of your generation don't even know who Miles Davis is, note that I said is, not was, despite his mortal death Miles' music will live on as long as Beethoven but ask your contemporaries about hip-hop, rappers wearing a garish diamond-encrusted cross, tasteless, flamboyant oxymoronic display as they blaspheme and excoriate women. Your generation has devolved into a morass of form without content."

"I still dig Miles and Mozart but just the

same, I want to…"

Dad wasn't finished. "Never did like the pop music of today mostly sticky whip cream which is why I evolved to real estate rather than playing such inane music at weddings and, don't forget son, you did minor in Business Administration and did very well which pleased me."

Mother assuaged, "And got straight A's if I remember."

"B-pluses and I minored at your urging, Dad, not my primary interest."

"Well perhaps you might be interested in how successful Harrison Real Estate has become and not-so-incidentally paying substantial tuition during your four years of college and I would expect…"

"For which I am truly grateful, believe me."

"And I was hopeful, after you had your fling as a writer or musician, you would join the firm. We presently have 14 diligent hard-working men and women in the firm, including your mother, and frankly, there will come a time when I will...well son, how does a Vice President nameplate waiting for Lawrence Dunbar Harrison with generous remuneration? Do you realize, son, that I started out as..." He was about to give his biography of choice which was overly redundant (which is a redundant expression in itself) as I have heard it too many times and apparently my mother heard it even more as she interrupted with a velvet shade so as not to hurt her man.

"And a good decision it was, Mason. Your success was beyond anyone's expectations and now look at us. An amazing man is my husband." She turned to me with an imploring tone, "Lawrence, you can wait a while before considering your father's generous offer, write, go into music, your taste and talent was not conventional. You never descended into the repetitive beats of three chord blues or two-beat rappers...you preferred the old masters. And the editorials in the student newspaper, even before joining your father's firm, you could probably intern at the Times, go for your Masters in Journalism."

"A far better choice for which we will be in a position to cover all expenses rather than you working in such a disparaging position at a hotel. I mean really!"

I didn't tell them that I do like some of the rappers like Kanye, Kendrick Lamar, Drake, D'Angelo. ("All we wanted was a chance to talk; 'stead we only got outlined in chalk.") Or the old great documentary blew me away, "Woodstock," Jimi Hendrix whom I actually liked more than anyone past or present but when I ventured such an opinion to my Father he read off the offense like a judge instructing the jury, "Mocking society, excessive drug use and death at an age where he self-sabotaged an expressive life. That's what happens to those who bow down to the devil!"

"Amen," Mother closed that chapter.

Father shared, "We almost named you

Miles but the Websters down the street beat us to it. You'd think with that last name they'd give their son, Ben, but no, Miles. What kind of name is Miles Webster? Whatever did happen to that boy?" Daddy was on a roll.

"Last heard he was with a nose-ring, a pony-tail, cohabitating with someone of similar gender living in a place called Port Townsend," Mom helped.

"Where's that? Upper New York?" Dad asked.

"No, I believe it's in Oregon," Mom said.

"No, it's in Washington, and I still love jazz and classical, but..." only to be interrupted by Father.

"And so in the face of your musical ear, my God Lawrence, you can nail the time signature and key after hearing what, twelve bars..."

"Eight."

"Eight. A gift! A gift for which you must be

grateful and never dishonor, you chose and note we supported said choice even in the face of disagreement when a person ignores a gift, a gift I say which is not a casual aptitude but nevertheless you chose to be a writer or so we believed and supported your aspirations and appreciated that even the Dean of the English Department, what's his name?"

Mother picked up the renewed energy as apparently the duet's break was over and they were playing their song once again, "Doctor Rothman."

I didn't know if it was intentional baiting or a mistake but I lightly fugue'd with: "Burg. Doctor Rothenburg."

And Father was once again comfortable with the rhythm of the attack, "Yes, him, he personally told me on graduation that you have excellent potential as a writer and now..." he made the motion of hitting a bell on a desk and calling in a stentorian condescending tone, "Boyyy!"

He got me with that one and I retorted in no uncertain terms, "I will be…I am a writer and it was he, Doctor Rothenburg, my faculty advisor, who suggested that I go out there and…"

"Where? Out where there?" Mom paradiddled.

And in the vein of a Jimi Hendrix riff on the Star Spangled Banner, I went for it with vintage Woodstock passion, "Out of my present protected environment, to have new and different experiences beyond my familiar comfort zones, to see, hear, learn about other people, experience other cultures…"

I was on a roll when Father interrupted with vigorous rationale, "You want to learn about other people, other cultures, join the firm. Our leading salesman, Abdomele Tochukwu is from Nigeria, our office manager, Chiyoku Daichi is from Japan, and our clients, commercial and residential run the gamut from the mid-East to China."

"And don't forget," Mother reinforced,

"Eduardo and Doroteia Emesio who just purchased, and we're talking a substantial investment, our Wilshire edifice which has been on the market for only a few months. Abdomele did a brilliant selling job beyond our expectations."

"There you go, Lawrence. You can't get more exposure to different cultures, genders, people than that. Join the firm...even part time so you can write about your experiences and..."

"Dad, I appreciate everything you say and your generous offer but...well, I need to do it my way...I mean what better approach to be exposed to the foibles of the human condition without...it's difficult to explain but, well, under the guise of service I'd be invisible and..."

To which Dad thundered, "Richard Wright claimed the 'Invisible Man,' but things have changed and no son of mine will ever have to be ashamed or walk with his head bowed or…"

"Dad," I pleaded, "I'm talking about being a

fly on the wall. The luxury of any writer is invisibility — not as an oppressive state but as a privileged exercise — to observe their world, their character, their behavior without them knowing I am surveying, recording, using as fodder, as material for my novel. What better way than to be anonymous which is a perfect cover, yes, as Courtesy Assistant to occupants of a particular nature in an almost covert residential high-end hotel?"

There was a glaring silence. I wasn't sure if it was an ending, an intermission or a closure that I might interpret if not with approval but perhaps acceptance. Father looked at my Mother who was chewing the left side of her lower lip as if it was black licorice. She paused and quietly asked, "Doctor Rothenstein suggested…"

"Burg…Rothenburg," I corrected not knowing if his name was an actual problem for her or if it was her way of getting me to bite.

Mom continued as if she was Inspector Clouseau claiming every purported error as part of the design. "He suggested you go to work as a bell hop? You are telling me that the Dean wants my son to be a all right, a Courtesy Assistant a rose by any other name still reads bell boy to me…he said that, Doctor Rothen…yes, burg, said that?"

Father feeling left out of this parlay and not fond of the omission, intoned, "It sounds like a Jewish suggestion, to me."

I had my diploma, emptied my student locker and went to Doctor Rothenburg's office for a closure of appreciation.

He was wearing a leather vest and a floppy bow tie as if it was part of a designated wardrobe for a PBS special airing on Sunday afternoon. Meshing perfectly with this outfit was a bemused expression precariously balanced between kindness and condescension. He was a Rhodes scholar who returned from England with outstanding credentials, three vests and an English accent (although he was born and bred in Connecticut.) Yet underneath all of that attitudinal veneer was a man of knowledge from whom I was able to learn extensively during my final year. He granted me his final personal lecture.

"Don't just hear, but listen! Listen to your inner voice and listen to theirs. Listening is the key. Don't just listen with your ears, listen with your intuitive perception which every decent writer must have, listen past your judgments, judgments are the assassins of creative artists. Save your opinions for the second draft and even then be very cautious lest you impose beyond the parameters of the event or skewed dialogue representing the writer's p.o.v. and not the character's. I detest when I read a character breaking their rhythm to express the writer's opinion, or stop the movement for editorializing, a venal..." He stopped as if late for a train, then, "Where was I?"

"You were accenting the value, the need to Listen."

"Ahh, yes, you were listening." He smiled to see if I got it. I did. "Yes, listen with your eyes and see which message their eyes are sending, messages of hope, despair, protection; listen to their body language which tells of past disappointments and vindictive victories. Hear what they say and listen to what is unsaid. The text is often evasive but the subtext, ahh the subtext, Lawrence, the subtext is always accurate. Listen with your nose and smell the illusion, listen with your soul to ascertain the authenticity or lack of thereof. That is the key source of a writer's trough. The ability to listen!" He paused either for thought or effect. It worked.

He continued in a whispered conspiratorial tenor meant only for blood brothers, "Choices." A mini-beat as if pending a breath of admiration. "What makes a man are his choices. My wish for you talented Lawrence is that you determine your choices by accessing your sentient, cognizant mind, redundancy intended." (As if he was grading his lecture.) "Consciously choose that which will challenge, confront, dare you to face a dangerous choice. Don't fall into the sweetened trap of nurture. Discomfort is not to be avoided. Open wounds can be a catalyst to discovery and unique expression. And pray do not mistake nurture as nature. Nay..." (pray and nay, his affectations were almost distracting from the valued content.) "Nature is amoral chaos. Nurture is salve for the ego's wound. What choices?" He paused again waiting for my response of acquiescence and silent applause.

I decided that I no longer was working for a grade or even sanction so I hurdled over the politically correct paradigms with, "Doctor Rothenburg, did you, I mean besides your doctoral thesis, did you write fiction, get published? I would like to read your work but you never mentioned it in class."

He stared at me to determine my motive. Perhaps I stepped over the line of propriety, that line of student/teacher, but then again, I graduated and had the right, although his inordinate stare did create discomfort.

"I was attempting to determine if you are being rude, no, please do not interrupt, I was attempting to determine if you are being rude, naïve, or sincere, Lawrence."

He held up his palm facing me, his hand indicating an officious traffic cop serving a busy corner due to a defunct signal. He preferred no response. Preferred? Insisted. He took a breath, let whatever it was that threatened to erupt, dissolve, a sad smile, a nod, almost like a public recitation of a pretentious preamble. "No, Lawrence, I have written a novel, actually three, and they are gathering dust along with one hundred and twenty six rejection letters. Ahhh, teachers teach, doers do. You were truly curious, I understand that. My suggestion of a path for you, for what I grok as an iconoclastic rebel underneath that respectful veneer, or is my perception amiss, Lawrence?" (In one of his lectures he cited two of his favorite American novels "A Thousand Acres," and "Stranger in a Stranger Land," the latter using the work 'grok' and

Doctor Rothenburg subsequently decided to use 'grok' "…as often as deemed necessary toward including this original word as an accepted part of our vocabulary.")

"I haven't made up my mind as to…well, my path, sir. Not yet. But I do intend to write a novel and get it published and…"

He interrupted, "Excuse a doting professor, young man but as I have an investment, so to speak, in your future…what I mean by that is that no one can teach talent, which you have most definitely revealed in some of your essays and short stories…but the good teachers, professors, carriers of truth can…and I, obviously sans humility include myself as one of the better ones, we can only assist the talented to access their gift. And, Lawrence, as you are a young man showing much promise, whom I believe has led a reasonably sheltered life, I ruthlessly encourage, urge you to have experiences that will test and confront, demand attention, awaken you to lives and issues which you have not yet encountered. Do not be a man dying of thirst next to a fountain. Yes!" He stopped and gleamed at me. I wasn't sure if it was a smile of encouragement or a call for praise. "Or," he hesitated with purpose, affording me the opportunity to nod eagerly, which I did but it was a rhetorical nod and certainly not eager as the thought of more years in the University was an anathema. "Or," he reconnected, "you can go out into the world, interesting phrase," he postulated as if grading his own paper, "…out into…a seeming paradox and yet it works!" It was apparent that he graded his paper with A-plus. "Yes, your choice to go out into the world in a Jack Londian fashion, have experiences of life, son, life's dangerous, wonderful, frightening, exciting, corrupt, transcendent adventures which all become fodder, grist for the mill, and please never repeat to anyone that I used such a well-worn cliché, which when you come to think of it, 'well-worn' is an unrequired redundancy when talking about a cliché, isn't that so, Lawrence?"

My nod this time was eager. Yes, I thought,

it is time to experience different and new…well, new to me, experiences. Not my Mother's or Father's expectations or even Doctor Rothenburg's, who despite his lofty airs, inspired, stimulated and facilitated my learning and growth as a writer, albeit unpublished as yet ('yet' being the operative word here.)

A Fly on the Wall

by Lawrence Dunbar Harrison

FIRST DRAFT [Per Dr. Rotherburg: first draft is to be a non-judgmental pouring out, unconditional vomit is not the word he would use but that's what he meant which means subsequent changes, i.e. editing, spell-check, rewrites, cuts, additions, etc.]

The names of individuals and certain edifices [find better word than edifice] have been changed to protect the innocent. [Ugh, what a cliché. Nobody is innocent...Correction]: To protect this writer and Publisher from legal action. Any similarity with living or dead people is strictly coincidental. [Another lie as the events, characters and dialogue are true to my personal experience. Discuss w/publisher.]

[Perhaps do prologue...personal, parents, influences, dedications...or just jump right into it...as a great writing coach once said "Every Story Should Start in the Middle of the Middle"]

DAY ONE   [maybe just jump in without "day one" or how about each chapter refer to the character?]

ANDREW:

Andrew, the Manager, "Follow please," led me to my locker as if it was Fort Knox. His rigid posture was what I imagined a dictatorial father's training of a son who was not as masculine as he wanted, ergo exceedingly rigorous. [ergo or thus...I like the feel of ergo when you say it?] My imagination may or may not be accurate, nevertheless it fits this writer's perceptivity. Or perhaps Andrew's unbending back may be a spinal defect. His neck was similar to a pick-up-stick used in kids' games, straight and remarkably narrow, topped by a head that was too small for his body adorned by a thinning moustache of such a dark hue a la black-on-lack that I wondered if he endowed it with shoe polish every morning as if he was from a rerun TV cop with a formidable stash which my parents watched. His attitude was imperious evoking a feeling that he was always looking down at people and as he was over six feet four and I was six feet with shoes on, his descending stare was not only physical but his disdain was more than that. I wondered if it was me, my persona which may have induced such or perhaps he was just establishing territory to the new employee, [or new kid on the block?] "Ah, here we be." (Be?) He did surprise me, however, as his head tilted, although the neck seemed thinly immovable, when he smiled. Although it was limited to his mouth as the eyes clouded showing no humor or for that matter any human warmth. His eyes were more like the black buttons of a fox. "This is your and only…" (he sometimes spoke in underlines) your locker, Lawrence. What do you prefer, Lawrence, Larry or…"

"Lawrence is fine, thank you."

The smile remained as if it was routinely glued in place at this particular time of every evening. "Lawrence it is. What after-shave are you wearing or is it some subtle scent? It's very effective."

"None. Just good old soap and water."

"Well, it all seems to, what's the word, serendipitous, yes, uhmmm." The smile gave the impression of a performer waiting for affirmation, of what I wasn't sure as I had no idea what he thought of as serendipitous or maybe he didn't know that the word meant a kind of creative accident and somehow I hoped that he didn't infer our meeting as such so I just met his smile with something between a grimace and grin and looked around to avoid what I could not define but certainly worth circumventing.

The basement room where our lockers were situated was not permeated with the usual dank noxious odors that I have experienced in the University cellar where Deborah Minkoff and I found a dark corner, she brought the blanket, skipping our English Lit class we made love or as Deborah said, "We're juicing like there's no tomorrow." But there was tomorrow when she told me she decided to drop out of college and go off with Alexis Weisman to, as she not so eloquently put it, "Explore other avenues of living." I didn't know what she meant until she clarified. "I decided to try being Gay, Lawrence, everyone's doing it, you should try, in any event Alexis and I are going off to probably Cambodia but first we have to stop off at her step-father's home in New Brunswick for some financial aid which for some reason she is sure he'll come through. Between you 'n me I think Alexis and her step-daddy are doing the nasty but that's none of my biz 'specially if it benefits her, well, us in terms of financial support, I'm all for it. Does that make me sound like a prostitute? If the shoe fits. So my sweet Lawrence not of Arabia, I'm off on a life adventure, if that's all right with you." Of course it wasn't all right, not that I was in love with her but I did enjoy and would now miss our clandestine cohabitations. No, this basement room of the Manchester Arms was clean, air conditioned, with wooden benches and mirrors.

He inserted the key and opened the locker, excuse me, my locker with a kind of elegant flamboyance short of a trumpeted fanfare. On a shaped wooden hanger was a black jacket with an S gold pin in the lapel, a red bow tie and a cell phone.

"Your size. 38 medium, although you look more tapered, you most likely will need the ability to move your arms freely on occasion, so if it's a bit loose that will serve you in the long run and," he smiled as if sharing a secret, "...in the short run, too, Lawrence. It's a wonderful name to say, very euphonic, rolls off the tongue so to speak." He did that smile again, as if it was waiting for an echo. I didn't rebound or resound. The pause was miniscule but my lack of response in that moment seemed to cause a chilled weather change. "The gold S in the lapel indicates staff a-k-a specialized service. The cell phone is calibrated only to one frequency. You may receive calls from staff and in the inner jacket left hand pocket there is a listing of the numbers of staff and function with whom you may want to page at one point or another. And the key, when you change, lock this securely, not that there is any concern for theft but we prefer lockers locked, perhaps that's why they're called lockers or is it the one with the key who is the locker, per se?" A sound emitted from his nose and chest which I assume was, well, an amalgamation of a chuckle and snort (I wonder if snorkel's derivation may be…) as he gave me the key with great solemnity, "Do not make a copy. If you should lose or misplace it, Ma," he snorkled again and leaned into me as if to share a sacred confidence, "Ma is what we on staff call the Manchester Arms, but again, Lawrence, only staff people refer to our home as Ma." I nodded although possibly not enough of an indication of worth for his clandestine sharing of Ma. He continued, "If you lose your key, Ma will charge you twelve dollars to change the lock and the key. And did you notice that door we passed down the hall?"

"Yes, I noticed the door."

"Good. That leads to our break room. For Staff only. Before your shift, meal breaks or every four hours you get twenty minutes. Coffee, water, magazines, no hierarchy, we are all equal in the break room in contrast to, oh well I am sure you understand. Questions?"

"It's all very clear. Thank you, Andrew."

That smile again. Too many teeth under the pencil thin moustache beneath hooded eyes. "Yes, good, I prefer Andrew. The diminutive usage of Andy does not quite do it, although I don't mind

Drew. But only outside of Ma. Perhaps over a drink. Do you like hot Sake?"

"I don't know."

"Either you like something or you don't."

"I never tasted Sake."

"Really." It was as if he dismissed me from any sense of importance on this or any other planet. "Ah, well, perhaps someday. Upstairs in ten."

He glided away leaving behind a sense of dismissal, disapproval and a faint aroma of perfume.

In the lobby Andrew viewed jacketed-me as if assaying a property for investment. "Hmm, very good. Well, Lawrence, your first Courtesy Assist assignment." A pause as if waiting for the appreciative recognition of a revered mission. Then he handed me a large bouquet of flowers, greens and other fauna I could not identify. "And," he signified with a discursive tone, "...Ms. Henderson and make sure it's Mzzz or she will be justifiably upset, Suite 403. She may request a particular assistance. Be at her service, Lawrence." I nodded and started away only to be stopped, "And Lawrence, a key characteristic of Ma's staff is the ability to listen to our residents. Not just listen to their requests but be an assiduous attentive listener as some rez, again our private term for residents who are exceedingly lonely and our courtesy is to provide them with, for lack of a better word, company and of course the best company is he who listens well. [Shades of Dr. Rothenburg's advice.] And as an aside but a remunerative aside it is, come Christmas some of our more generous residents leave a handsome gratuity to individual Courtesy Assistants, so listening, Lawrence is not only a compassionate gesture, it can also contribute to our end of the year largesse. Notice I said our. Each Courtesy Assistant tithes to the manager, namely yours truly, twenty-three percent of any gratuity. Understood?"

"Yes."

"Any problems, issues with what I have just confidentially shared?"

"Eminently clear, Andrew, and totally acceptable."

"Excellent. Ms. Henderson is a retired actress but never use that word in her presence. The last employee of Ma who referred to her as retired is no longer with us. She often has a need for an audience. Give her a good review, Lawrence, and come Yuletide the stocking will be burgeoning. Burgeoning, don't you love that word. You can almost taste it. Burgeoning." My lack of response was noted. "Go...but oh yes, just remember when you see Ms. Thing, thirty four."

"Thirty four, what?"

"Thirty four," and his turned back was met with my unseen shrug. Thirty four.

Ms. Henderson

I knocked. No response. I knocked again. No response. I stepped back, checking the door number, 403, right, I knocked once more, stronger, and heard, "Enter." Her voice wasn't so much an invitation but more of an authoritarian reward, a grant to the deserving from...Mzzz. Henderson.

She was reclining on a chaise longue otherwise known as a couch to we plebeians. But part of my initiation into staff was a little red book of instructions and nomenclature such as: chaise longue, not couch; appurtenances as in accessories and equipment; vase pronounced vahhhz; garbage as refuse; perspiration never sweat; bathroom as lavatory or rest-room; toilet as commode.

She wore, no, not wore, but was adorned in a flowing lilac chiffon that not only covered her difficult-to-define body but practically the entire...

"You're new."

"Yes, Ms. Henderson. Shall I put these in water?"

"You're a good looking young man."

"Thank you."

"What a banal response..." as she imitated my "thank you. Why thank me? I had nothing to do with it. You should thank your parents, your genealogy, your ancestors, there are better replies when someone expresses appreciation. For example, tell me I am beautiful."

She was not but I knew the play. "You are beautiful, Ms. Henderson."

"Yes, I know." I smiled at her response. "Notice, young man, no thank you. Do you thank Van Gogh when you are stunned by his starlit nights? You should thank the gods that you are in the presence of such artistry, or in this case, such beauty."

I nodded ineffectively and muttered, "Would you like me to put these in water?"

"What you see young man is a beautiful woman somewhat older than you but beauty ages well in this particular body as the gods graced me.

Grace is the Deity's rare gift of sublime generosity."

'Grace' reminded me of my father's comments but not nearly as florid as Ms. Henderson's. Her words sounded like they were lifted out of bad movie. And maybe they were.

She snarled a contemptuous sound as she ranted simultaneously posing as an unjustly wounded star my mother loved, Joan Crawford or maybe it was Bette Davis, "He said stop playing hard to get. I am not playing, I am hard to get." A quick adjustment to an angry mourner, "Ah my young man, if you only knew. My past is littered with failed erections of those men who underestimated me including one particular husband who did not have the dignity of a donkey with Lymes disease and made love...love? He fucked," She glared as if in confrontation, "Does that word challenge the polite parameters of your presentation young man?" She tossed her hair theatrically, "Not even Gandhi was always Mahatma Gandhi. No matter. Karl was his name, Karl fucked like a monkey, a chimp who comes within 7 seconds. And he had his socks on. How rude."

I felt like I was watching a freshman drama club in college doing an unpublished Tennessee Williams play and recalled Andrew's and Dr. R's listen-advice, and so I adapted a façade of an interested, attentive listener, which was not all that difficult as Ms. Henderson 's grande damme performance with surprising dialogue bordered on weirdly interesting.

"He had the backbone of a roasted marshmallow. A coward in sheep's clothing who lawyered me to near-penury!" She talked, no launched words as if she was righteously attacking an enemy. "Nobody takes away all that I have danced."

She stared at me awaiting my applause as I am sure that last line came from a straight-to-video movie starring hers truly. The best I could do was nod, smile and say, "You are a most impressive woman, Ms. Henderson. These flowers?"

She rose with ponderous grace as her - I suppose I might call it a gown - preceded, receded and covered her arc. She leaned in, close to me, a little too close for comfort. (Isn't there a song like that, "Too close for comfort...") She took the flowers from my hands, not-so accidentally brushing her fingers slowly on my wrist, smiling in an implicit subtle sensuality which was not as subtle as she assumed, "How old do I look, young man?"

Andrew resonated loud and clear. "Thirty-four I would guess, Ms. Henderson."

She giggled like a child-actor doing a bad audition for a dirty-old man producer, looked at me with feigned amusement, "And how old are you, young man?"

"Twenty-two, ma'am."

She grunted a scathing sound, grabbed the flowers out of my hand, stomped in her bared feet and garishly painted toe-nails to the kitchen area with her chiffon clearing a path on all sides, "The next time you call me ma'am will be the last service I require from you and I shall so instruct your supervisor whose name I believe is Arlen."

"Andrew."

Standing by the sink, putting a vase underneath the spout. "Men do not know how to arrange flowers." And she stopped as if lost in a curtain call. In a soft voice to the gods, "He was special...after sex was un peu de la mort...it was wonderful...almost cruel." Her reverie was cut short by the splashing water into a jar.

"Will there be anything else, Ms. Henderson?"

"There are more anything-elses than a twenty-two year old pup would grasp but on your way out you may adjust the I know it's not a thermometer but I forget the suitable word."

"Thermostat."

"Well, you're not totally useless."

"What temperature do you prefer?"

"Now is that a cue or is that a cue! Do you know what cue line means young man?"

"I prefer you elucidate, Ms. Henderson."

"Elucidate. A recent college graduate I would guess. Major in English, correct? That's a rhetorical question because I know I am obviously accurate. Have you seen any of my films? 'Raging to the Abyss,' 'Close to the Edge', 'Howard's Hide-away?'"

"Not yet but I shall..."

"No you shall not as they are not available on Netflix or On-Demand or in fast going-out-of-business video stores. I have one of the few copies. Perhaps some evening when you are not on duty we can have the pleasure of watching them. Champagne and caramels will be served."

"Sounds wonderful, Ms. Henderson, but I signed an agreement which not only guarantees confidentiality but specifies no socializing with residents."

"Well, we can confidentially work things out, young man."

"Thank you but I'm afraid I'll have to pass on that generous offer."

"You're not afraid at all. Words, words. Waste of time. My movies, transferred to a DVD which lacks the stark quality of film. Film. No longer a commodity. Everything is now done of Video. Digital shmigital, it ain't film. What a loss wouldn't you say? You look confused. A cue, young man, is that line in a script...you know what a script is?"

"Yes, for a movie or stage-play or TV..."

"TV," she condescendingly expelled air as she was cutting the tips off the bottom of the flower stems, "I watch TV for reality shows which are staged realities because in life those fools would either be in jail or an institution but I confess that I do find them amusing. A cue, my twenty-two year young man is a line in a script for a movie, a movie, a film, what is your name?"

"Lawrence, Ms. Henderson."

"Good name." Then she said it like a fading announcement only missing echo. "Lawwwreennnnccce. A brilliant movie. One of the greats. Peter O'Toole, the most beautiful, talented, foolish man, oh we had some times. Did you see 'Lawrence of Arabia,' Lawwwrence?

"Yes, two times. I love it."

"Well, there's hope for you yet. A cue, Lawrence, is a line that sets up the next character's line...like what temperature do you like? And my character would respond to said cue with, hot hot hot." She triumphed and dropped the flowers into a huge vase, turning to stare at me as if she gave me a cue line to appropriately, or rather inappropriately respond. I did not pick up my cue. I said nothing.

She dismissed me following the flow of her chiffon back to the couch, oops, chaise longue, "Acting is obviously not your field. You may leave as soon as now comes to mind." She arranged her formative body, picked up a remote and I heard the TV, "Why do you think your wife hit you with the frying pan?" I eased out.

[find better word than eased]

BREAK ROOM: [use or cut...can accomplish this without title maybe]

I was on a twenty-minute break when I walked into the Break Room which looked like a TV set for teachers in between classes. Andrew was sitting at a table drinking something while reading a magazine. I went to the huge coffee urn and was about to move the lever to pour when I heard, "Unless you're ready to donate a kidney I wouldn't recommend it." I turned and Andrew motioned me over, "Bring your cup."

I walked over and in response to his welcoming gesture I sat down as he lifted a private thermos, "I hope you take it black because ..."

"Yes, that's fine, thanks. You bring your

own coffee, do you?"

"Manny, the man in charge of coffee, water, and sundries for the Break Room brews about eighty-cups in the morning and by the time most of us are on a break, it tastes as a rancid as a dead cat's fur ball, he said waiting for the question."

"The question? What question?"

"When was the last time you tasted a dead cat's fur ball?

I smiled, nodded, sipped, "This is very good. Thanks."

"I grind the beans myself, every morning."

There was an uncomfortable silence as my prior contact was all business with his supercilious attitude but now Andrew was, well, convivial. "I had an interesting time with Ms. Henderson."

He held up his hand in a kind of gentle rejection. His fingernails were manicured, polished neutral glistening. "Break Room unwritten rules:

We do not talk business, raise our voices or use our cells."

"Ah, sorry, okay."

"No problem, you're new in the game." He picked up his magazine, "Interesting article in here about John Updike. Do you like his work?"

"Actually, yes, very much. He nails America's small town ethos."

"His definition of a grown man is a failed boy."

"That's very good."

"Yes, it is. Have you ever read this magazine?" He held up Frontiers.

"No."

"Of course."

"Of course?" [Talk about a condescending dismissal.]

"Well, Lawrence, I should have assumed that a man who never tasted Sake would not be into

Frontiers. It's a gay magazine."

He paused for some response which I obviously did not give.

"Does that bother you?" he asked.

"No."

"That I am gay? Does that bother you?"

"No."

"Are you sure, Lawrence?"

I tried to lighten the load, "As long as you don't hit on me, no problem...Andrew."

"And if I do?"

"It would be a waste of time."

He smiled with gleaming teeth that matched his nails. Turned to the magazine.

"Well, my break is just about over," as I stood and left.

[stet or rewrite/add the additional dialogue that did take place... for more back and forth...good dynamics between the two?????????]

He smiled with gleaming teeth that matched his nails. Turned to the magazine.

"Well, my break is just about over," and I stood about to leave.

"No, it isn't. You still have twelve minutes." He turned some pages of the magazine, stopped. read and looked up, "Can I ask you a personal question?"

"It depends."

"On what?"

"I have certain, what's the word, parameters I guess. Certain personal information about myself I prefer to keep personal."

"His ego is covered with appropriate lace. No, as intriguing as it sounds I am tempted to pry but no, Lawrence, I was going to ask you a question referring to me."

"Okay. Go for it."

He looked at the magazine and then held it

up revealing an ad showing two photos, before and after of a nude man's butt, with copy: Brazilian Butt Lift, $5,000. "The question I was going to ask my personal protective pal, I know we're not pals but I couldn't resist the alliteration."

"Your question."

"He's attentive, yes, my question." He stood, lifted his jacket and did a slow one-eighty revealing tight-fitting pants, "Do you think my butt needs a lift?"

I burst out laughing. I love to be surprised. He smiled and sat down. "You have a wonderful laugh, it's infectious. Well, do you?"

"No, Andrew, your butt looks just fine."

"Oh, you've been scoping out my butt have you?

"I fell into that one."

Silence a few beats and then, changing the tone of our ping pong match, leaning in asking me conspiratorially, "Tell me, Lawrence, what is a college graduate doing at Ma working as a Courtesy Assistant?"

"You said we don't talk business in the Break Room."

"More a personal question than business wouldn't you say? There is something unsaid, an elusive subtext to your presence and this particular man is interested. In you."

"Are you hitting on me, Andrew?"

"You said it would be a waste of time."

"Yes."

"Being an efficient manager of my time, Lawrence..." he said my name as if it was edible, "...but as an inquisitive, sensitive man I am more than curious because you do not fit the standard mold of Ma employees."

"Simple," I lied, "...my degree in Liberal Arts hardly qualifies me for a position in the commercial world and I need a job."

"That simple, hmmm?"

"'Fraid so."

"I don't believe you."

I shrugged, checked my watch, "Well, my break really is over. Thanks for the coffee," and I left.

[keep or end as previously indicated?]

Sr. Gutierrez

He looked like a clown late for a children's party, nevertheless he was an impressive man not only because of his stature which did call attention to itself [itself??? or himself?] as he was only about 5'2" with a huge head and a sizable moustache which reminded me of an ancient movie with Brando, "Viva Zapata." It was his voice. A tone of a frog on a holiday [crazy imagery and I like it...keep or rewrite? Dr. R said that a line or phrase may be brilliantly written but if it draws attention to itself taking the reader out of the flow, cut it...not yet] A tone of a frog on a holiday that effortlessly emanated from a barrel-chest with resounding authority. His voice was singularly fixated on his world in which any subject of his focus must match his unique frames of reference. Adding to it all was a torrent of non sequiturs but then again to him they may have been part of his interior configuration. [I'm getting ahead of myself...perhaps let the scene play out and demonstrate the aforementioned...cut???]

Holding the newspapers and magazines I brought to his suite, I didn't know if he was addressing me or just taking inventory. "New York Times, Wall Street Journal, New Yorker, Rolling Stone, Time, Mother Jones..." he tossed them onto a huge table constructed out of a tree log with knots remaining. He stared at me as if I had committed a crime. "New York magazine?"

I pointed to the table, "There it is with a tree on the cover."

He picked it up and held it facing me with

the third finger of his left hand covering the tree. "This is the New Yorker. Not the New York magazine. Two entirely different publications. New Yorker great journalism. New York good crossword puzzle enabling me to win the self-awarded gold-star as I fill out every mother's white blank space. An important silent victory in a world too noisy to notice."

"I'm sorry. This is the package Mr. Trumble at our stand gave me specifically for you."

"Well, Mr. Trumble missed it which is not the first nor shall it be the last but you might take notice of the publications required by yours truly, can you do that?" He paused waiting for me.

"Now?"

"Yes, now."

Looking at the publications splayed on the table I said, ""New York Times, Wall Street Journal, New Yorker, Rolling Stone, Time, Mother Jones... and I will check with Mr. Trumbull about the missing New York."

"Missing magazine is not your fault but from here on in as of now it will be your responsibility."

"Yes, sir."

"I do not respond well to the officious bureaucratic 'sir'. Do you know who I am?"

"Yes, s...yes, Mr. Gutierrez."

"Wrong answer."

"You are Mister Garcia Gutierrez, aren't you?"

"If someone with an attitude of arrogance, insolence, defiance says do you know who I am...the appropriate reply, appropriate if you have the cojones to do you know who I am...is I know who I am and that is enough."

I nodded, trying to sublimate a smile, "I'll check on the New York Mag," and started to go.

He stopped me with, "No, not yet. We are just about to get involved in a discourse."

"I'm not sure what you want me to do or say, Mr. Gutierrez?"

He surprised me with, "How tall are you?"

I stopped, "Six foot give or take a half an inch."

"And how tall am I?"

"I would guess, well, somewhat shorter than me give or take."

I wasn't sure if he laughed or derogatorily grunted, "When did you learn to be so diplomatic?" He walked to the small fridge, taking out two bottles of beer. "Negro Modelo, good for the kidneys and the mood. Join me."

"I'm sorry Mr. Gutierrez, it's forbidden for an employee to..."

"You always pay attention to the rules, acquiesce to what is acceptable and evade that which what is taboo?"

"No, not always."

Holding up a bottle towards me, "Then about now being not-always. Join me in hiding from history."

I was intrigued by what he meant by 'hiding from history' but..."Thanks but I don't think so."

"What time do you get off?"

I checked my watch. "Five minutes ago. You're my last tour."

"Since you're off duty, if you refuse a man's offer to share una cerveza, in Madrid you would be considered rude to some, others perhaps an enemy."

I folded. "Okay...but on one condition."

"Digame, hombre."

"Even off duty I'm not permitted to socialize with residents so..."

"You're not socializing...you're serving a resident who requests your presence."

"Only on the condition that you keep this

confidential. If the manager finds out I'm out of a job."

"Confidencial, el secreto hombre, secretos shared with two men...a good thing...compadres honoring a bond." He handed me the bottle and clinked it in toast, "Salud y pesetas y una muchacha con buenas tetas."

My school Spanish didn't entirely go to waste as I understood, clinked the bottle and yes, he's right, Negro Modelo is good beer. Very good.

"Now tell me...como se llama...what is your name? When compadres share a drink a name is needed."

"Lawrence."

"Good. Now, tell me, Lawrence, what ultimately convinced you to break the rule?"

"I want to know what you meant when you said to join you in hiding from history."

"Ayyy, he listens, good." [Again, Dr.

Rothenburg would be proud.] He cascaded in a torrential verbosity with the energy of a hot mountain stream. [...conflicting images as mountain streams are cold but perhaps that may be the pay-attention-intention of this imagery.]

He cascaded in a torrential verbosity with the energy of a hot mountain stream. "History is past manifesting in the present demarcating our future. History is a thug with a bad limp imposing its rank breath on our desensitized Pinocchio'd noses reminding us that history does not exist to nurture but to harm within formulaic chaos which is an oxymoron giving us the apparition of choices which may cause obesity, diabetes, cavities and corporate profits concluding of course with the need to digest the debris or kill our neighbor when his dog keeps peeing on our porch. History puts a badge on a man who shoots and then busts you for bleeding on his uniform. History is the Department of Justice citing you for conspiring to conspire. History is the Pentagon's DARPA, Defense Advanced Research Agency with the sole sanguinary mission to dominate the world. You have skin in the game, Lawrence? You think you haven't even ante'd up in this dire contest but the day you incarnated your hand was dealt. No doubt you will stick and play your cards close to your best which will not be good enough because history's deck is stacked and the house always wins. By choosing to share this moment, compadre, una cerveza is smashing history in it's iron-clad balls when Lawrence said fuck it I'm breaking the rules and will live with the consequences. That, mi amigo, is hiding from history. Salud."

He clinked the bottle to mine and we both imbibed as I was assimilating his raucous rant. I looked at his loft and wondered why he has three computers, many notebooks, post-its with scribbles I could not define when he interrupted my sight-seeing, "You have a question?"

I felt caught in the act but the Negro Modelo loosened my defensiveness, "Yes, what are all those computers about?"

"Writing and research."

"Writing?" I was a little too responsive, not wanting to reveal my subliminal purpose as Courtesy Assistant, "How interesting" I covered with neutrality, "Care to share what you write?"

He looked at me, hard, as if he was determining if I was an ally or an enemy, then rose and got two more bottles, giving me one, clinked our bottles. I expected a toast but he surprised me with, "When I said writing your insides bounced like a punk teen-ager dropping a water balloon from a six story roof." I just drank and shrugged. "No, if we're to be compadres sharing secrets and beer, I need more than that."

I was tempted but not ready, "Sorry, yes you're very perceptive..."

"Don't bullshit a bullshitter."

"It's just, yes I was, okay intrigued that you're a writer, for personal reasons...but well, I'm just not ready to reveal my...my plans I guess you would call them."

"Everyone has a plan until they get punched in the face. You know who said that?"

"No."

"A brilliant man called Mike Tyson."

Trying to detract from his question, "Another brilliant man said, You got to be careful if you don't know where you're going because you might not get there. Yogi Berra." I nodded, smiled, still feeling his pressure to reveal.

"I peeped your hole card, young man," he said with a wicked grin. "You're an aspiring writer aching to someday write the great American novel. Yes?"

"Like the young man said, I'm not ready to reveal. "

"Are you ready to be slaughtered by castrated critics?"

I said nothing in the face of his accurate perceptions insisting to myself at least that I would not affirm my ambitions.

"Clive James review of a Brezhnev memoir: 'Here is a book so dull that a whirling dervish could read himself to sleep with it and birds would fall stunned from the sky.'" He roared an evil glee. "I love that motherfucker who sliced up Brehznev in such gallant erudition." He glared demanding an affirmation. "Come on, Lawrence, talk to me. Admit that under the Courtesy Assistant badge is a rankling writer aching to come out." And then he imitated a brat of a rat chant, "Come out come out wherever you are." He looked at me as his eyes softened to almost admiration. "He ain't talkin'. Gotta' respeck dat."

My curiosity was relentless segueing into an avid interest hoping my redundancy would get him off me. "What do you write on your three computers?"

His eyes demanded my respect, "I trade not telling your boss about breaking the rules with you not revealing to any living sentient being which is superfluous because if you are sentient you are alive but then again most living people who worship at the altar of mediocrity are not sentient and do you think I lost the thread? No, Lawrence, we make an agreement written in metaphorical blood. Neither one of us reveal what is shared in this moment. Deal?"

"Deal."

He offered his hand which I took as his powerful grip held longer than expected. Letting go as if he won an undeclared contest he said, "On computer one, I write porn." He paused for my response as I smiled, nodded a pitiable attempt at being sophisticated, a vague cover to my naïve reaction, "Porn? Really?"

He laughed. "Weak cover, kid. Yes, porn which substantially rewards this man as they not only sell online for a decent fee, they are also adapted to film, or rather digital, more remunerative. Give it up, Lawrence. Inside you are freaking out."

"No, not freaking, just a kind of, what's the word, almost hilarious to be so, well...surprised. Computer two?"

"I write social political blogs. It's not that power corrupts. No, it's the corrupt who lust for power. My blogs reveal the hypocrisy of the powers-that-be. Under a pseudo, encrypted not to be traced as occasionally it has been used to evoke protests and change. Not always for the better."

"But why different computers? Just stack one with big time ram holding different files that will..."

"No. There is a particular energy in my choices. Depending on my theme, each computer is a waiting friend with a particular energy inviting me to dive in beyond circumstances, considerations or judgments." He whispered as if I was part of an agreed-to conspiracy, "'Be regular and orderly in your life, so that you may be violent and original in your work.' Flaubert. Get it, young Lawrence?"

"Okay, yes, I'd like to read them?"

"Which?"

"Your blogs."

"Not the porn?"

"Well..." I drifted off into silence.

"Your 'well' speaks."

"And the third?"

"A long, very very long, suicide note. The fact that I am still here talking with you indicates there is more to be written."

"Suicide!" I was startled. "Is that a metaphor or..."

His eyes raged and voice fired up with an escalating positive power in direct polarity with what he was saying.

"From the moment we're born we are preordained to die. Death is the end-game although many wealthy self-absorbed imitations of a human being try every trick, fad, or Swiss medical device to delay, elude or even freeze the unavoidable conclusion. No one escapes. Bust me for dilating the trite and obvious. Oh surely everyone ignores the destiny of the deal; fight with your wife with your husband with your kid, go online to divert and distract from the waiting truth, disappear into a seductive escape called virtual reality but reality sans virtue always intrudes. Listen to me, Lawrence," he boomed a domineering ultimatum, "Irregodamnedgardless of the power plays of the malevolent puppeteers, snatching defeat from the jaws of victory, reality always intrudes." [...yes, sometimes he talked in bold] He took a swig of the beer, laughed loudly but without joy. "A mockery of searching for authenticity, self-sabotaging in a delirious suckle on the imitative pacifier of circumvention. They induce harmful impositions as meaningful but despite their planet-earth authority parading as supremacy, it is a meaningless game with the royal straight flush already in hand calling the bet. End-game. The house wins. You die. What difference does it make if someone dies a miserable death in a private room in an upscale Jewish hospital with tubes in every orifice or..." he paused checking to see if I was still with him, which I was mesmerized in an almost hypnotic attention, "Choosing a more elegant departure of my own time-line..." He let that hang while I was still dealing with his brilliant rationalized declaration of intended cessation of life. Then, "No comment mi escritor secreto?"

"I'm still dealing with your justified declaration of suicide and wonder if..."

"You're generation Lawrence, alas and cognitive caring alack, you're not getting it. Einstein knew even way back. 'Technological progress is like an axe in the hands of pathological animals.' "

"I can't buy into that hopeless forecast quite yet. Enormous progress has been made on the positive side to..."

"False optimism is just another form of real stupidity. And Lawrence, you are not a stupid young man but it is time to learn that that there is a fine line between sticking to your guns and being killed by a gun."

"Just the same there are options in our life that..."

He shook his head and looked at me with kindness, "Compadre, you're not getting it. Your generation is sucked into smart phones without being smart, thinking that a cell with all the apps money can buy will make you happy. Camus said 'Sometimes happiness feels better than truth.'"

"My generation, me and my friends, we're not blind to the realities of the world, to climate change and we are actively looking for solutions in order to..."

He interrupted, "Don't you think it's strange that world peace is in the hands of five nations who are the world's main producers of weapons?"

"Of course the contradictions are formidable..." I felt like I was on debate team in school. And losing.

"Are you religious?"

The question startled me, "Uhmm no, not in the...what you would call the standard, belonging to a church-way."

"Believe in God?"

"Yes but again not in a...the biblical definition of God. I think of not so much God as that heavenly dude with a flowing beard but a Spiritual power that..."

"That doesn't give a shit about what we do or don't do. Say that out loud and you're defined and defiled as an heretic who is doomed to hell which of course is the dark bribe forcing parishioners to tithe ten percent of their paltry income not knowing that in the Bible's original language hell was the name of a garbage dump and the poor people who could not afford a casket and a decent burial were thrown on top of the garbage dump...thus hell." He shouted to the Gods, "Calamity to the infidels." And then looked kindly at me, almost paternally. "Oh, Lawrence with his not-so-hidden naïve young optimism does not realize that we on planet earth have lost our harmony."

"I still believe...well think that we, yes, those of my generation do not have to be doomed to..."

He hurled a heated hot spear of a whisper at me, "The world has been, is, and always will be eternally fucked. Why? Because there is no cure for primal paranoid tribalism!" He stopped suddenly. Took a few gulps of beer, wiped his garrulous mouth, smiled, and as if we were bosom buddies sharing life histories in the comfort of trust without rancor and in a surprising casual voice, "I come from a small town where my smallness took notice. It was front page news when they opened a pink Berries so when I got into a fight and bit the leg of a six foot six tall Neanderthal it was a bizarre headline in the Newton News, Garcia goes ape! Oh, Lawrence, never underestimate stupid people who are in power."

"Sounds like the Newton News could get some mention in computer number two."

"Years ago I did just that. The editor, per his monthly column as a Christian was against gay-marriage. I revealed for his readers that same editor was having an affair with the 21 year young mild looking proof-reader who just so happened to be of the Muslim faith and of course the male gender. The community forced the paper to close." He paused, shook his sizeable head, "It did not give me as much pleasure as I anticipated." He stood, walked to one of the computers and said, "I need to be alone now."

Home: I was in my spacious room typing the end of my meet with Garcia Gutierrez when I heard my father call up, "Son, mother and I would like a word." Like a word. Who talks like that? My Father. Particularly when he is about to lay something pejorative on my butt. I sighed and steeled myself for some unbidden advice or new guidelines, another word Dad used for non-negotiable rules. Did I forget to take out the garbage. I laughed at this memory and now, well, I was no longer a teenager so it was not fear that guided me downstairs but morbid curiosity.

As I was about to enter the living room he called, "In the kitchen." Whew, must be serious because anything heavy that might impact our lives was always deliberated in the kitchen.

He was sitting at the table as Mother brought a tray of brownies straight from the oven, cutting them up in slices, keeping very busy as a justified effort for avoiding eye contact with me. Father indicated a chair. I sat. He said, "We'll wait until mother finishes."

To which she said over her shoulder, "Oh don't wait for me, Mason, just make like I'm not here."

"We'll wait, mother."

And so we waited in an oppressive silence

until Mother came to the table with a plate of sliced brownies. She was about to sit but remembered and got many paper napkins which she distributed in front of each of us as if that is the reason for this gathering. "Hands get sticky but these brownies are your favorite, right Lawrence?"

"Yes, mom." I nibbled, "Ummm delicious."

"You haven't tasted one, Mason. I think you'll love them."

He ignored his wife's nervous distractions from the agenda which obviously they both knew and I was about to be included. "Lawrence, you are now twenty-two years old. An adult. What does being an adult mean to you, Lawrence?"

"Dad, what's going on, what is this about?"

"An adult," he said as if it was a cherished state, "is responsible for his choices and everything that goes with it."

Shades of Dr. Rothenburg defining a man

as a series of his choices. "Yes, Dad, I own being an adult." I was tempted to smart ass a crack but mother put her hand on my wrist sensing silence was a better option and to just hear him out.

"Good," he continued, "And as an adult your Mother and I have discussed possible options for you to choose, as a life path or pattern, if you will."

If you will. Jesus he is really into something deep by formalizing an oration.

"As you know we were pleased to be in a position to totally fund your college education including room and board perhaps amounting to forty-eight thousand a year," (No, not 'perhaps' with Dad...exact). He continued, "Times four years that amounts to approximately one hundred ninety two thousand dollars." (You can bet it was not approximate.) "A considerable investment in our son and my ability to do so reflects the substantial success of Harrison Real Estate."

"To which I am enormously grateful, Dad,

you know that."

"Yes, we do. Now, Lawrence, now as an adult there are significant decisions to be made."

"What are you getting at, Dad?"

Mother pushed another brownie my way and whispered or rather cooed, "Just hear your father out, Sonny."

I nodded and put a lid on it as I was ready to do battle with anticipated new ground rules. I was too old for that.

"What I'm getting at," he continued, "is our distinct disfavor regarding your choice to be a...and yes you call it Courtesy Assistant, and I call it a menial server which is hardly a successful reflection, a poor return of our four year investment, wouldn't you say?"

"Your investment so to speak, Dad, has considerable promise for, as you say, a reasonable return but it may take some time before my work is published, and until then you must know that I am enormously appreciative for all that you have..."

He wasn't buying, "Not only financially, Lawrence, but even of more impact is that it distinctly and disturbingly slaps us in the face of our values. Harrisons have not, are not and will never be servants."

I got it. My father's turning up the heat and his grateful son must ...there's that word again...make a choice to his father's liking. "What are you telling me, Dad?"

"Choices. You can choose to go to graduate school for your masters, majoring in, I prefer Business Administration..."

Mother gently chimed, "But Sonny is such a good writer, Journalism would be fine, too, wouldn't you say?"

"All right yes," Dad conceded, "And work part time in the firm or not even go to grad school," his energy transformed into an oration of hope and promise, "... but choose full-time and join my firm which one day will be our firm which one day will be your firm. We're growing, Lawrence, in good economic times and with wisdom even in poor economy, Harrison Real Estate is expanding and relative to our success and validated by the business community I have been approached by investors, legitimate corporations to participate and/or sell the company for sums beyond expectation. Join us, Lawrence, and we will make an impressive team." He concluded with a huge smile, proud of the defined possibilities, expecting total obeisance.

I wondered if my breathing was audible as I inhaled deeply trying to control my emotions which were close to being out of whack because I knew the alternatives. "And if I choose to continue my path, my choices, my way as an adult to enhance the sources of my writing?"

"As a servant?" he boomed.

"As a fly on the wall observing characters and behavior...Dad we've been through this. Don't you want your son to cut the cord, to be his own man?"

"By being your own man...yes, all right, do you know what that means?"

"I'm sure you'll tell me"

"Don't smart-mouth me, boy."

Mother put her hand on his, "Sonny's just trying to..."

He wasn't buying. "What it means, Lawrence Dunbar Harrison, if you choose to continue your life as a servant, it will not be in this house."

The bomb dropped and I retorted, "Either this adult accedes to his Father's wishes or he is evicted. Is that what you're telling me?"

"What adults do, son, is yes, leave home, get an apartment, get job, handle finances that their parents took care of for twenty-two years, yes."

Mother implored, "Sonny, we do not want you to leave. Please, find a way to make it work for you and your father."

"Understand, Lawrence, if you choose to leave our home where your mother cooks and prepares your meals, even handles your laundry, where I pay for your car insurance, no rent, no gas or electric bills, if you choose to, I repeat, cut the cord, be aware my young adult son of the benefits you are forfeiting and the significant responsibilities of an adult on his own."

"What's the timeline on this eviction notice?"

Mother looked back and forth at each of us, "Please, there must be some compromise that will..."

"I expect a decision within two weeks."

"Four," mother implored.

"Four it is, Mother wishes. And son, if you choose to leave, of course our firm will be of help in finding a suitable apartment and we will continue to pay for your car insurance the remainder of the year."

"Can I come by for a Sunday dinner occasionally?"

"Being snide is not helpful, Lawrence. What I am suggesting is that you seriously consider your options. Total support financially and if you go to Grad school, work part or full time in my firm, have life experiences other than being a servant and write, yes, whereas if you continue living at home with all the favorable options even including, yes, the back staircase for an occasional guest, you are a healthy male adult after all, as long as she, and in these times I am grateful it is a she, but she does not sleep over."

Mother smiled trying to make peace, "Oh I would not mind a sleep over and serve breakfast to you and your girl friend."

I mumbled, "Waterloo."

"I didn't hear what you said, Lawrence."

I stood. "I'll give you my answer, my choice before four weeks." And walked out.

Sitting in my room, pissed, angry, close to rage, about to rage downstairs and say, "Fuck it. You can take your firm and..." but I stormed out. To where? It mattered not as I jumped in my car, which yes, my father bought for me and covers the insurance. I drove. Not to any destination. Just drove through the furies that were about to implode.

After thirty minutes on the road fortunate that I didn't have an accident or get a speeding ticket, I returned home. Went up to my room ignoring that my parents were watching TV in the Den. In an organized fury I opened the files of everything I have written on "Fly on the Wall," spent hours editing, rewriting, spell-check...and compressed the file with proper heading. Went online, Googled, researching literary agents, independent publishers. Wrote an introductory letter accompanying the first sixty-seven pages of my novel, ending with Mr. Gutierrez, suggesting, "You may be interested in the first half of my novel. If so, please do not hesitate to contact me re a potential arrangement.   Sincerely   Lawrence   Dunbar Harrison."

I figured to get bite before my eviction.

Or not.

Actually recalling Dr. Rothenburg's three unpublished novels and hundreds of rejections I am apparently being naïve in "getting a bite"...but bite or no, it's time I leave the Daddy-domineering-nest regard...or   as   Mr.   Gutierrez   said, irregodamnedgarless of the supportive securities.

Gentle knock on my door, "Come in," and Mother entered with a tray of brownies.

"Peace offering, Sonny."

"Oh, Mom, I have no issues with you."

She mock-whispered, "Daddy is washing the car. He buys a new top of the line Cadillac every year. For cash. He can well afford to have it washed but no, he insists on doing it himself. That's your father."

I smiled, shook my head, "I remember at

least a decade ago when I was invited to wash the car with him. Fun at first until he kept busting me, You Forgot the Bumper, the Headlights Need More Than a Swipe."

"Sonny, Daddy has his ways but he is a very very good man. Please, Sonny, know that he cares for you. His invitation for you to join the firm was not out of malice..."

I interrupted, "Invitation? It was a do-or-die, accept-or-else."

"You don't have to decide. Four weeks... and if you need more time I'm sure I can get Daddy to relent and..."

"No, Mom, more time is not necessary."

"You made up your mind? Already? Maybe you should give it, I mean let the heat...let everything cool down and in a couple of days or even weeks you may be in a better position to..."

"It's a done deal, Mom. "

"You're not quitting your job as ... yes, Courtesy Assistant?"

"The job is only a symbol, actually an opportunity for both of us. For Dad to continue to dominate his son and for yours truly to claim, as Dad kept reminding me, make an adult's choice and everything that comes with it including what doesn't come with it."

"You're sure? You will move out?" Tears filled her eyes.

"Yes, and it's not like I'll be out of touch. Just out of Daddy's grasp and learning how to deal with life on my terms."

She nodded and handed me a bulging envelope. "Daddy doesn't have to know that I have been putting away some money over the years for a special occasion."

"Mom, that's not necessary, I'll find a way to..."

"Yes you will find a way and you my first born will always be a special occasion for this mother. This will help you get started, you know, furniture, microwave, food in the fridge..."

I accepted, hugged her. She looked at me, touched my face which evoked cell-level memories of when I would freak out as a kid she would caress my face through the tears until I calmed down. She said in a quiet reserve of strength which was not heard in front of her husband, "You're making the right choice for a young man. I'm proud of you. Turning down all that support and comfort to be on your own. It's not going to be easy, you know."

"As Dad reminded me when I hated doing math, 'If life was easy cows would have wings and money would fall from the trees.' No cows, no money trees, I'll handle whatever has to be handled, Mom."

"I know you will. You're a strong young man who will, well, Sonny, we don't have to tell Daddy about this visit."

"I love you, Mom."

"This is ...well difficult for me, your presence in my life from the day you were born is the most important thing...and...well, Sonny, I mean I respect that you...well maybe just please give it a little more time, and think of other possibilities, I mean...oh God, I really don't want you to leave, I mean maybe we can negotiate with Daddy to alter the ultimatum. Perhaps you may want to give it just a little more time to consider everything."

"Mom, I am no longer interested in washing Daddy's Cadillac."

www.ingramcontent.com/pod-product-compliance
Lightning Source LLC
Chambersburg PA
CBHW070518200726
48293CB00007B/2591